A Noteworthy Enchantment

JEANNE HARDT

Abby & Alex —

I hope you
enjoy this!

*Jeanne
Hardt*

Chapter 1

A Voice Beyond Compare

All of the fluttering nervousness in Alesa's belly finally subsided. If only she had been this calm for the entire song, but at least she could be at her best for the closing lines.

She bravely donned a smile for the king, drew in a large breath, and let the high notes soar. "*And the beasts of the wood knew all that was good.*" She held out the word, *good*—the one that hovered at the pinnacle of her vocal range—and let the note carry and fill the palace dining hall. "*And they bowed before their king.*" She slowed the last verse to a conclusion, then gave her own bow to the king *and* queen.

The newly married, royal couple applauded, and soon after, the entire room erupted with shouts of praise and thunderous applause. Alesa peered around at the series of long tables filled with the elites of Shanavar, all dressed in their finest clothes. The women donned elaborate jewelry like nothing she had seen before. Their precious stones glimmered, reflecting off the many candles that lined the center of every table.

Never did Alesa imagine that she—a simple peasant—would be lauded by such prominent people.

"She has greater talent than Zeborah," a woman said.

Alesa snapped her head in the woman's direction, and their eyes met. The woman cast a gracious smile, and Alesa's confidence magnified. To be compared to Zeborah overwhelmed her—and not just *compared*, but proclaimed better than she. Zeborah had been said to have the most exquisite voice in the realm.

Alesa returned her attention to King Lorin and Queen Odette. The enthusiastic cheers in the room had not diminished in the slightest. It felt as if even the marble floor beneath her shook from the exuberance.

King Lorin held up a hand, silencing the crowd, and looked right at her. "Come closer." He waved, beckoning her nearer.

Her heart fiercely beat as she stepped toward the royal table. The room had quieted to such an extent that she could hear the swish of her long, emerald-green gown as she walked. Her mother had spent too much on the silk fabric for the dress, but she had insisted Alesa looked like she belonged in the palace. "Yes, Your Majesty?"

"You were brilliant." He smiled at her, then turned to his wife and patted her hand. "Was she not?"

"Oh, yes." Queen Odette spoke with sincerity and sweetness. "Your voice rang true. I have never heard anything quite so pure and resonant."

"Nor have I," the king said. "Your mother did not lie when she told my esquire that you have the finest voice in the realm."

Several people in the room gasped, and Zeborah's name resonated through the air. Surely, they had the same thoughts as Alesa. Until now, Zeborah had been the only woman ever asked to sing for the king. The words of both royals honored Alesa, but perhaps Zeborah's friends feared their compliments might upset her.

Alesa darted her eyes around the dining hall, searching for Zeborah and praying she was not present. Alesa never wanted someone's feelings to be hurt.

"Thank you for your kindness, Your Majesty," she humbly said. "It was my honor to be here."

"And it will be *my* honor to invite you again. What say you? Will you afford us the pleasure of your songs on another occasion?"

"Whatever pleases you, Your Majesty. I am a loyal servant." She offered a second bow. The day had exceeded all of her expectations.

"Very well." The king clapped a single time and one of his manservants appeared at his side.

"Yes, Your Majesty?"

"Escort this lovely young lady to her family's table so she can eat. She has more than earned her supper."

The servant bowed to the king, fanned his hand, and inclined his head for Alesa to follow. He led her to the table where her mother and sister were already seated. Farrah appeared troubled, yet in contrast, their mother appropriately *beamed* as Alesa approached. Her elation was not surprising, since she had not only properly dressed Alesa, but she had also arranged the performance through the king's esquire. King Lorin had taken pity on the widow of one of his soldiers and agreed to allow them passage into the castle.

The servant pulled out a chair for Alesa. "M'lady."

She eased onto the seat, and a new kind of excitement rushed in. Just as she had seen on all the other tables, their own overflowed with food: roasted meats, cheeses, sweetbreads, assorted vegetables, and plum pudding. Her favorite.

Mumbling and animated whispers surrounded her, but she chose to focus on her family rather than the crowd. She wanted them to revel in the experience with her.

Farrah twisted a strand of her long, strawberry-blond hair around her finger and sharply blinked several times while staring right at her. "You sang disappointingly well."

Alesa gaped at her sister, completely at a loss for words.

Their mother huffed. "*Disappointingly?* Shame, Farrah, for saying such a thing. Be proud of your sister for giving an exceptionally *fine* performance."

"It will only get her into trouble." Farrah leaned across the table. "Alesa, you should have done as I suggested and sing off key." Her sister substantially lowered her voice. "Zeborah will not be happy, and I fear what she might do to you."

"*Do* to me?" Alesa shook her head. "I assume you are troubled by those silly stories you heard about her. You should have better sense. Disregard those tales and listen to Mother and me. All those anecdotes of magic and sorcery are foolish. Those things do not exist."

Farrah's eyes greatly widened in fear, and she gulped.

Alesa turned to see what had frightened her young sister.

Zeborah.

The most beautiful woman in the kingdom glided toward their table. How could anyone fear such a regally tall and glorious woman? She wore a lavish, purple gown—a color normally worn only by royals. That fact alone showed her esteem. Her raven-black hair cascaded down her back in a long, intricate braid, woven with shimmering strands of gold.

Her nearness brought a feeling of instant intimidation. Before now, Alesa had only seen her from a distance.

Zeborah smiled down at her. "What an astonishment you are. You must be *proud* of your voice."

"Of course, she is," her mother blurted out, before Alesa could utter a syllable. "She has been singing since infancy."

"Truly?" Zeborah licked her ruby-red lips. "May I assume you have always enjoyed hearing her?"

"Yes. Her voice brought delight to my husband as well before his passing. Honestly, after losing him, her singing brought me comfort in my darkest days."

"That is so …" Zeborah placed a hand to her heart and tipped her head to one side. "… *touching*."

An unexpected chill washed over Alesa. She shivered.

Zeborah pivoted and stared straight at her. "Why have you grown quiet? You brilliantly filled this hall with your musical notes, which proved you have a voice. Have you nothing to say, or are you only able to *sing*?"

"I—" She gulped, trying to come up with what to say to someone of her stature. "I appreciate that you came to our table and said such kind things. Although I have not heard you sing, I was told *your* voice is the one to be admired."

Zeborah grunted. "Why should anyone admire *my* voice, when our king has just proclaimed yours to be the finest in the land?"

Alesa's heart thrummed hard, and she let out a nervous laugh. Zeborah had not outwardly stated any sort of jealousy or hurt feelings, but something in her eyes—along with the unladylike *grunt*—told Alesa that was exactly how she felt. She found herself in an awkward position.

What do I say now?

She had to tread lightly and not stomp on Zeborah's questionable emotions any further. "The king merely repeated what my mother had said. Do not all mothers believe their children are the best at whatever they do?"

"I suppose. Yet, our king is not one to repeat what he does not himself accept as true. Be *proud*, Alesa." She bent to her level. "Wear your voice well." Zeborah's lip twitched ever-so-slightly. She stood erect, tossed her head, spun around, and walked away.

Alesa kept her sights glued to the woman, all the while pondering her remark and the steely tone she used while saying it.

The king's brother, Prince Chadwick, crossed the floor, and Zeborah hastened to him. She latched onto his arm and lit up with a radiant smile. The prince returned it with much less enthusiasm.

Alesa released the breath she had been holding. "I know Zeborah is upset over what was said about my voice, and it concerns me."

Her mother reached over and squeezed her hand. "Do not be troubled by Zeborah. As you can see, she has already forgotten the whole affair." She jerked her head toward the pair in the center of the dining hall. They conversed in low tones, and occasionally, Zeborah lightly laughed. From what Alesa could tell, nearly every eye in the room lay on them. They had become the new spectacle.

They made a handsome couple. Zeborah possessed undeniable beauty, and the prince was a prize all women craved. Tall in height, strong physique, and a face chiseled with perfect features. Alesa admired him, yet she had the good sense to realize he was not for her. His heart belonged to someone else.

Zeborah kept a firm grip on the prince and guided him in the direction of the hallway that led outside. They got to the door's archway, and Prince Chadwick glanced back over his shoulder. He frowned, looking at one of the maids.

"Oh, my," Alesa whispered. "Did you see that?"

Her mother nodded. "Poor Jenessa. It is well known that the prince loves her, but Zeborah is determined to keep them separated. From what I have heard, Zeborah has complained to the king that the maid is beneath his brother and is pushing His Majesty to encourage Prince Chadwick to wed *her*."

"Is the prince unwilling to stand up for his heart's desire?"

"I believe he *fears* Zeborah," Farrah earnestly said in a hushed tone, then peered around them. "I heard that her skill at sorcery grows by the day. Some feel she should be banished, but King Lorin refuses to do it."

"Banished?" Alesa folded her arms. "Because of rumors? Our king is honorable, and he will not bend to the whims of gossip. Besides, he has a sense of obligation to care for her."

Farrah scowled. "When will you allow yourself to grasp the truth in the stories told? As for his indebtedness, it should have ended long ago." For a girl the age of twelve, she was certainly opinionated.

Their mother shook her head. "Some carry the weight of debts to their deathbeds."

"It was not King Lorin's debt," Farrah persisted. "It was his father's, and the details of what actually happened to Zeborah's parents are conflicting. And yet, because of what was perceived to have taken place, Zeborah has free rein in the castle. I agree that our king is honorable, but he is also blind to the evil taking place within his walls."

"Evil?" Their mother huffed. "That's enough talk of nonsense, Farrah. We should be celebrating your sister's accomplishments." She gestured to Alesa's full plate. "Why are you not eating?"

"I keep thinking about what Zeborah said. Something in the way she told me to *wear my voice well* caused ice to run through my veins. What do you suppose she meant?"

"Ice?" Farrah lifted her chin high. "I told you, she is evil, and those feelings you had are proof of it."

Their mother waved a hand in dismissal. "Foolishness. All I heard from Zeborah were words of praise. She admires you, my dear." She lovingly patted Alesa's cheek. "Would it not be splendid if the two of you sang together one day?"

"I suppose…"

Farrah grunted.

"There is only one woman in the realm who needs to be concerned over what Zeborah might do." Their mother wiggled a finger, pointing to the other side of the room. "Jenessa. She would have the right to fear repercussions from Zeborah if Prince Chadwick follows his heart and chooses her for a bride."

Alesa looked back at the maid who bustled about, clearing away dirty plates. If the prince honestly loved her, why had he not placed her in a finer position? Perhaps to keep their relationship a secret?

No.

Everyone in the realm knew about it. Gossip about the royals spread even faster than other wild rumors. Hopefully, the man was not a cad toying with *both* women.

Jenessa kept her head high, although Alesa knew her confidence had just been tested. She had witnessed the man she loved being fawned over by Zeborah. Regardless of Jenessa's low stature, the prince could select any woman he wanted for a wife. Both women were lovely—though Zeborah was fairer—but true love required more than pleasant looks. The prince had to gaze beyond their outward appearance and delve into their hearts, where one was sure to be broken.

"Oh, my!" Alesa clutched her chest. Zeborah reentered the room—*alone*—and went directly to Jenessa. Zeborah leaned down, said something in Jenessa's ear, then stepped away. The high-statured woman glanced at Alesa before ambling off. Her eyes held something much darker than admiration.

Like before, an icy chill cascaded from the top of Alesa's head and flowed through her to her very soul. Surely, her sister's remarks had ignited unnecessary caution. As their mother had stated, it was all foolishness, and Alesa needed to discard every ounce of worry.

"Jenessa looks as if she might cry," Farrah whispered.

"She has the right." Alesa's chest constricted. "I can only imagine what Zeborah said to her. Even the kindest of women can behave in an ugly manner when vying for the same man."

"What do you imagine she did with the prince when they left the dining hall?"

"None of us should even be contemplating that. The realm needs no more rumors." Alesa picked up her fork. "We should eat."

"I agree." Their mother grabbed a piece of bread and took a bite. "Delicious."

Farrah leaned back in her chair. "I cannot eat." She studied Alesa with the saddest-looking eyes. "I love you, and I fear for you."

Alesa set her fork aside and reached across the table to her sister. "I love you as well, and I promise, there is nothing to fear." She cast a smile, but it did not alter her sister's demeanor.

Strangely, Alesa's belly roiled with a different sort of anxiousness.

What if Farrah was right?

Chapter 2

Enchanted

In utter darkness, Alesa sat atop her down mattress, hugged her legs to her chest, and rested her head against her knees. Although dressed for sleep, she could not even close her eyes.

This should have been the greatest day in all her seventeen years, yet her stomach's unease had not lessened. Even the good food she had consumed only magnified her discomfort.

They never had such a feast in their simple cottage. They ate enough to get by, but nothing came to them in abundance. Not since her father died in the war. Her mother's only hope for a better life for her, and Farrah, was to see them married well.

Alesa sighed, not wanting to think about marriage. Love often brought heartache, and she could not erase from her mind the image of poor Jenessa's turmoil. If only she could revisit the elation she felt when she so perfectly hit those high notes and let everything else vanish from her thoughts.

A glimmer of light came into the room, and Farrah entered, holding a lantern. "Mother told me I needed to come to bed, but I see *you* cannot sleep, and I doubt I will either." She set the lamp on the small table that sat between their two beds, then climbed up onto hers. "Shall we talk about what happened earlier?"

Alesa shrugged.

"I hope you can forgive me," Farrah went on. "I should not have behaved so badly. You sang wonderfully, and if not for my fears of Zeborah, I would have relished it. I just wish Mother had never approached the royal house to offer your service." She twisted a strand of hair around her finger—a habit she could not break. "Please do not be upset with me. I only want to be sure you have heard all that has been said about Zeborah."

"Why are you so persistent?"

"Because I want you to be careful—*guarded*."

"To stave off an evil enchantment?" Alesa sarcastically asked.

Farrah frowned and nodded. She looked as though she might cry.

"Forgive me, Farrah." Alesa moved to the edge of her bed. "I can see that this is important to you, so tell me what you have heard." She had a strong inclination that she would not like what her sister had to say, but because of her love for Farrah, she would endure it.

Farrah wiped her eyes and sniffled. "Will you listen with an open mind?"

"I will. I promise."

Farrah released a shaky breath. "I know you are familiar with Lady Ellen."

"Yes. The woman who is incapacitated."

Her sweet sister wrinkled her nose. "That means unable to walk, is that not so?"

"Precisely."

"Well, prior to her disablement, she was a beautiful dancer. Similar to your performance tonight, the king's esquire enlisted her to dance for one of the royal banquets. The next day, when she rose from her slumber and stepped out of bed, the bones in her legs cracked beneath her, and she fell to the floor. She screamed in pain, and her chambermaid found her lying in a heap. The healers say there is no explanation for her condition."

"That is horribly sad," Alesa whispered. "I cannot fathom the agony she has endured, but what does Zeborah have to do with Lady Ellen's torment?"

Farrah scooched to the edge of her bed and faced Alesa square on. "Zeborah also danced for the king. From what I was told, she was there the night Lady Ellen danced. She praised Lady Ellen for her talent, but those watching them say that Zeborah despised her for it. They claim jealousy flowed from her like water. She does not want anyone outdoing her in *anything*." Her gaze bore deep into Alesa's eyes.

Alesa understood her intensity. "I know why you fear for me. You have pointed out the similarities. Still, I do not believe any human can cause someone else harm by simply wishing it so."

"She does not use simple wishes. Zeborah collects unusual herbs and the blood of rare beasts. She uses them to practice her sorcery and cast spells. Some have said that they have heard her mumbling enchantments from her chamber. One of the servants claims he came upon a strange bluish-purple mist seeping from the crack under her door. He breathed some of it in, before he had the good sense to leave, and it made him light-headed. The servants in the castle have every right to fear her. My heart tells me that Zeborah is evil."

"Hearsay is not proof. If she does indeed collect blood, I find it disturbing. Even so, I cannot accept that she is capable of *magic*."

Farrah scoffed. "You say that, but I know you well. When you spoke of the chill she created inside you, you were afraid." She lowered her head, then slowly looked up again. "You *should* be afraid. Do you remember what happened to the miller's wife?"

"Are you referring to her loss of hair?"

"Yes. She had the loveliest, silken hair—and this account is *not* hearsay. I witnessed it myself. I was at the market, and I overheard someone praise its beauty. The following day, every bit of the woman's hair fell out. I remembered seeing Zeborah in the market as well, and without a doubt, she heard the comment."

Farrah reached over and grabbed Alesa's hand. "She thrives on being the best at everything. My heart has revealed much to me in Zeborah's regard, and it tells me, she is coming for you. I fear she will make you mute."

Farrah's distress permeated the small room and dove straight into *Alesa's* heart.

Mute? She trembled, and it angered her that her body reacted in such a way. "I refuse to be afraid. I must hold tight to my belief that magic does not exist. Unless someone actually touches me, I cannot be hurt. Incantations are not real, they are merely utterances used to invoke terror. They cannot create *physical* harm. They toy with the mind—just as the thought of them alone has caused you unease."

Farrah stood, crossed over, and sat beside her. She put an arm around Alesa and leaned into her. "I wish I could believe that, because I do not like feeling this way." She tipped her head back and met Alesa's gaze. "I have never feared for you more." She encircled Alesa with both of her arms and cried.

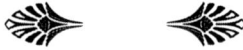

Once again, complete darkness surrounded Alesa. Farrah had cried in her embrace for a great length of time, until exhaustion overcame her, and she stopped. Alesa had tucked her sister into bed and extinguished the lantern, and now, Farrah's shallow breathing affirmed her slumber.

Alesa had assured her sister that their dog would alert them if anyone came near their cottage, and it comforted Alesa, knowing Bo slept curled up by the front door. Still, her overactive mind would not let her rest.

She kept envisioning the miller's wife and Lady Ellen. Had it been a coincidence that they had lost the very thing that made them special? Since Alesa did not believe in magic, coincidence was the only explanation.

Stop tormenting yourself!

She lay flat on her back with her hands folded at her waist and burrowed her head deeper into her pillow. Time ticked by, and her eyelids grew heavier and heavier…

In the silence of the still night, Alesa found herself peacefully drifting. All of her anxiety faded.

"Wear your voice well…"

Zeborah's words reverberated in her mind, and the same ice-piercing chill she had created before rolled over Alesa's body. She shivered, and her blankets gave no warmth. She tried to sit up to grab the spare quilt at the foot of her bed, but she could not move—not even to open her eyes. Her lids would not budge.

Too, too heavy.

Something bitter covered her tongue. Her body shook—convulsed—like it never had before. She panted rapid breaths, then repeatedly swallowed, trying to wash away the wretched taste.

I must wake from this dream!

The peace she had momentarily felt, vanished. Even in sleep, fear tormented her.

She squeezed her eyes tightly shut and forced her thoughts to shift to happy things: Bo chasing butterflies. Multi-colored spring flowers. Pleasant afternoon rains that brought about brilliant rainbows.

Her breathing slowed, and her mind rested.

Much, much better.

The nightmare vanished.

Alesa woke to the delightful chirping of a bird, and she smiled. All of the night's worries had been for naught.

She yawned, sat upright, and stretched, reaching her arms blissfully high.

What is this?

Instantly, her heart constricted. A bluish-purple residue covered her quilt. She braved touching it and found it to be a chalky powder. Memories emerged of what Farrah had said about the servant seeing a bluish-purple mist under Zeborah's door, and thoughts of the dreams she had just experienced joined them.

Wear your voice well...

Zeborah's voice echoed in her mind. Was it a memory from the woman saying it to her at the king's meal or from her dream? Or, had she actually heard Zeborah speak the words in her room?

"*Farrah.*" Alesa slapped a hand to her own mouth. Why had her sister's name come out in song?

Alesa cleared her throat. "*Farrah, you must wake.*" She pinched her lips together. Like before, she sang every word. Had she not forced herself to stop, undoubtedly, she would continue on into another measure.

"What are you doing, Alesa?" Farrah sounded groggy, but her words were normal and *spoken*.

Alesa kept her mouth shut, afraid to answer.

Farrah eased into a sitting position and gasped. "Where did this come from?" She pointed at the chalky substance. "It is everywhere." Her eyes fearfully widened, and she rasped staggered breaths. "Zeborah was here! Was she not?" She rubbed her temples. "My head is pounding. What did she do to us?" Her poor sister trembled atop her bed, yet gazed frightfully around as if afraid to move from it.

Alesa could remain silent no longer. "*To us, I do not know. To me, I fear I do.*" She passionately held a hand to her heart. "*She did not take my voice, but covered us in goo.*" Alesa rolled her eyes. The substance on them was not *goo*, it was a fine powder. Not only could she not stop singing, she was forced to rhyme—*horribly*—and with feeling.

Farrah fearfully studied her. "Why are you *singing?*"

Alesa swallowed hard. "*I cannot help but sing and let its cadence ring.*" She fanned her arm in dramatic proclamation.

"You are enchanted! I feared Zeborah would make you mute, but this—"

Their mother burst into the room, holding a broom. "The floors are covered in purplish-blue chalk! Even Bo has residue in his fur." She eyed the beds. "I see it is here as well. What could have caused such a nuisance? It will take hours to clean, and I have a severe pain in my head. Hurry and dress. We must rid our home of it."

"Mother." Farrah carefully pushed her covers back, stood from the bed, and approached her. "Zeborah was here."

"Zeborah?" Their mother laughed. "That is nonsense. Bo would have barked had there been a stranger in our home. Why do you say something so foolish?"

Surprisingly, Farrah had calmed a great deal. She frowned and rested a hand on their mother's arm. "This substance that has you perplexed is the same color that I was told came as a mist from beneath Zeborah's door in the castle. The servant who told me said it made him light-headed when he breathed it in. I believe we inhaled so much of it that it put all of us in a deep sleep—even Bo. I, too, have an ache in my head."

Her sister had always been wise for her young age, and she posed a sensible explanation. Still, Alesa did not want to accept it.

"And what of you?" Their mother looked right at her. "Does *your* head ache?"

Alesa shook her pain-free head.

"So, you are not unwell?"

Farrah cut her eyes in Alesa's direction. "Show her."

Alesa took a big breath. "*I feel quite fine, but my voice is not mine.*"

Their mother grimaced. "Why are you singing?"

"I asked her the same," Farrah interjected. "She cannot help but sing. The only explanation is enchantment."

"Ridiculous!" Their mother soundly tapped her foot. "You girls are playing a game that I do not appreciate. And to go to such lengths as to dust the entire house with this—this substance—"

"*Say no more, Mother.*" Alesa rose from her bed, clasped her hands to her bosom, and theatrically posed. "*Farrah speaks true. I cannot stop singing or rhyming to you. Zeborah said wear my voice well, and I am. I sing loud and clear and the best that I can.*"

Her mother stared at her in frightened wonder, then leaned the broom against the wall and slowly crossed to her. "You truly cannot speak normally? Or behave as you used to without all the drama?" She gently cupped Alesa's cheek. "Have you tried uttering a *single* word?"

"*Yes.*" Alesa covered her mouth before any additional words spilled out with cadence.

"This cannot be." Her mother dropped down hard onto the edge of the bed, sending a cloud of colored dust into the air.

"Hold your breath, Mother," Farrah said through a hand clasped to her own mouth. "Or you might inhale more of the substance."

"*I doubt it still holds power*," Alesa crooned. "*It has diminished by the hour.*" Unable to hold her emotions in any longer, she openly cried.

Farrah put an arm around her. "Please do not weep. I feared she would take your voice entirely. You sing beautifully, so this is not such a bad spell."

"Not bad?" Their mother rose and dusted off some of the colored residue from her skirt. "For years I have denied the existence of magic—regardless of all the stories I heard. And now, my denial has brought a curse upon my sweet girl. Had I been open to the possibility of it, I may have seen it coming. Yet, surely it will not last forever. If it does, constantly serenading and rhyming like a troubadour will lead her to madness. Not to mention what it will do to those of us who have to continuously listen to it and watch her dramatics."

"But Mother," Farrah persisted, "you told Zeborah that Alesa's voice brought you joy and comfort. How has that so quickly changed?"

"She is not herself." Their mother sharply nodded. "That is how. I cannot bear to listen to her when she voices her thoughts in such a nonsensical manner."

Alesa cried harder. Her mother and sister carried on a conversation as if she was not even there. She sighed through her tears. If she tried to join in on the discussion, it would only worsen matters.

"Oh, my…" Her mother moved closer. "Forgive me, my dear. I should not be so harsh. But you must understand—until this very moment, I denounced the mere idea of sorcery. And seeing you this way…"

Alesa looked her in the eyes, chin vibrating, but did not respond.

Her mother stood exceptionally tall. "We shall go to the king and demand that Zeborah be made to remove this wicked spell."

"It is unlikely he will believe Zeborah cast it," Farrah said. "His heart is soft where she is concerned."

"I will make him see reason." Their mother marched toward the bedroom door, spun around, and faced them again. "Get dressed. We must hasten to the castle." She scuffed her foot through the dusting of powder on the floor and glanced at the broom. "Cleaning can wait."

Chapter 3

Seeking Aid

Alesa gazed down at the brown fabric of her linen dress—nothing like the elegant, silky gown she had worn to sing for the king. Today, she looked like the peasant she had been since her birth. She never minded living in the village, yet having had a taste of royal life made her wonder how different her world would be had she been born to an elite.

Her father had not ranked high enough in the king's military to afford their family better circumstances. If only he had been born into privilege and dubbed a knight. That would have changed everything.

Her heart wrenched at the recollection of her father. He had been proud to serve the king, but it ultimately resulted in his death. She missed him every day and wished now more than ever he had lived to help her through the awful circumstance she had found herself in.

Her mother marched in front of her along the dirt road. The dear woman's determination warmed Alesa to her core. She always put her and Farrah ahead of herself, making her the best parent imaginable. As much as Alesa missed her father, she admired her mother's increased strength as a widow. Her sternness often came across as harsh, but Alesa knew it was based in love.

Farrah lifted the bottom of her long skirt and increased her pace, putting her beside their mother. "What if the king will not see us?"

Alesa had wondered the same, but did not attempt to voice it.

"He will see us." Their resolute, confident mother jutted her chin high. "I will not be denied."

They continued on in silence.

A stroll to the castle could not have been more perfect on such a gloriously lovely day. The sun comfortably warmed their surroundings, and the sky held no clouds or threat of rain. Even so, Alesa's heavy heart kept her from fully enjoying the beauty of it. Her simple—mostly pleasing—life had become entirely different overnight.

She gazed at the faraway, snow-covered peaks of Mount Ashalon. The bright white gleamed against the rays of sun that beat down upon it, yet did not manage to melt it. One day, she hoped to travel to those distant lands and learn for herself what it felt like to be surrounded by dense, snow-covered forests. At present, all her hopes seemed pointless. She did not want to go alone, but who would ever agree to journey with her and be plagued by endless crooning?

Then again, maybe the curse had already ended. She needed to find out.

"*It is a lovely day.*" The enchantment did not even allow her to frown at the realization that she remained under its spell. Her face formed a smile of its own volition. "*And I must not dismay.*" She sang with fervor and glee.

The second she stopped, she folded into herself, trudged along the road, and moped. It struck her that she would be forced to behave as a showpiece whenever she opened her mouth and lent her voice to any sort of conversation.

Farrah peered back at her and pushed out a concerned-looking smile. "It *is* a lovely day, and you need to hold onto hope."

Alesa merely nodded.

The road began its incline leading to the castle. Her father had explained long ago that it had been built on the highest hill in Shanavar for the sake of protection. From the castle walls, the entire vastness of the realm could be seen, easily alerting the guards to the presence of anyone approaching.

They neared the wall that circled the castle and moved closer to the enormous entrance gate. The night before, it stood open. Today, it was sealed tight with guards posted at both sides.

A mighty fortress.

One of the guards brandished his sword. "What business have you here, peasants?"

Her mother boldly advanced. "I seek an audience with the king—along with my daughters."

The man chuckled. "You deem it that easy? Why should I grant you entrance?"

"We were here last night—welcomed by the king. My husband, Enwood, served in his army—*your* army. Surely, you remember him."

The two guards spoke in low tones to one another, then the one who had addressed them stepped forward. "Enwood was a good man, yet that alone does not afford you an audience with the king."

"Please. Tell King Lorin that Bithia has come with her daughter, Alesa, who sang for him." She gestured to Alesa. "A problem has arisen with her that requires his aid."

The guard glanced at Alesa, so she cast a genuine smile.

"I heard of her talent," he said. "The king was quite pleased, and there has been much talk of her ability." He faced her mother directly once more. "What sort of difficulty shall I relay to the king?"

"Alesa…" Her mother roughly cleared her throat. "…has been enchanted."

The guard cautiously studied her, grabbed the other man by the arm, and the two took several steps away. They again put their heads together in conversation.

The second guard pivoted toward Alesa and eyed her up and down. "We have determined that you appear to be perfectly well. Is this a ruse?"

"Certainly not!" her mother fumed, then huffed. "I am an honorable woman, and I would never waste the time of my king."

The first guard pointed at Alesa. "Stay exactly where you are and tell me of this enchantment."

Farrah gave her an encouraging nod.

Alesa deeply inhaled. "*There is no need to fear, I come to you in peace. Lend me now your ear, my singing will not cease.*" She opened her arms wide and gazed at them in earnestness. "*Enchanted, that I am, I cannot speak at all. I sing the best I can, and to your beckoned call.*"

The two men exchanged confused and far-from-humored looks. They mumbled to each other, and Alesa swore she heard one of them say, *Zeborah.*

The taller of the two moved closer to Alesa's mother. "I will go to the king. You and your daughters are to wait here until I return."

"Thank you." Her mother curtsied.

The sign of respect was normally given only to the elites, yet perhaps she was showing him the same courtesy, hoping to gain his favor.

He opened the gate—just enough to go through—and immediately shut it again. The other guard protectively stood in front of it. The guards treated them nothing like the way they had the previous night when they had been ceremoniously welcomed.

Farrah took hold of Alesa's hand and gave it a squeeze. "Everything will be all right." Her words did not match the fear in her eyes. Although her sister had not said it, Alesa assumed she might be thinking the very thoughts she had been pondering. *If they angered Zeborah, would she do something worse?*

The gate slowly creaked back open.

"King Lorin will see you," the guard boldly stated and pushed the opening wider. "I will escort you to him myself."

Farrah kept hold of Alesa's hand as they proceeded into the courtyard. Their mother proudly walked at the guard's side.

They passed several ladies roaming the grounds near the gardens. Just as the women had looked during the meal the night before, they wore elaborate dresses and jewels as colorful as the flowers in the many manicured beds. The ladies of the castle most assuredly lived their lives in leisure.

Whispers from them fell on Alesa's ears. "She is the one Zeborah hates," one of them plainly said.

Hates?

A strong word for perceived jealousy, and if true, why did Zeborah not make her mute? That would have been a significantly crueler punishment for her talent.

They continued through an expansive archway and into the high-rising castle. Alesa held great admiration for its magnificence and the unique structure of its rounded turrets. Yet, it was not as warm and inviting as their cottage. It may have been exciting and a place she hoped to visit often, but knowing Zeborah could possibly appear at any moment made it much less appealing.

The guard led them up a circular stairway in one of the turrets. Even the stones of the walls seemed less attractive today. *Everything* felt colder.

They reached an upper floor, and he proceeded down a long hallway that opened into the high-ceilinged throne room. It was void of furnishings with the exception of the king's gold, tall-backed chair and the queen's smaller throne beside it. The royal seats perched on a raised platform at the far end of the room.

King Lorin sat comfortably in his place. He watched them approach, all the while stroking his long, full beard. Oddly, the man was alone. No queen. No other guards.

Where were his servants and protectors? Alesa had been told the king conversed with his subjects in this particular room, but she assumed he would at least be surrounded by advisors.

The guard halted in the center of the floor and put up his hand to stop them as well. "Your Majesty!" he bellowed. "Bithia and her daughters, as you requested."

"Very well. You may leave us."

"But Your Majesty—"

The king's eyes widened, and the guard bowed and strode from the room.

Alesa's mother stood utterly still as if not knowing what to do. The huge, majestic room swallowed them, and Alesa felt entirely out of place. Surely, her mother did as well.

The large tapestries covering the walls caught Alesa's attention. They depicted battles and festivals, the designs intricately woven in an array of hues. Everything in the room was larger than life, and the king himself seemed more *above them* and out of reach than he had been in the dining hall. Something about the fantastic gold throne and overpowering setting made him so.

"Come closer," he said—just as he had the night before—and bade them near with the wave of his hand.

Her mother came to life and confidently proceeded toward King Lorin. Farrah urged Alesa to move, and they joined her. They placed themselves several paces from the king.

He sat taller. "My guard spoke of an enchantment." He said the word as though *ordinary*. "What say you in this regard?"

"You believe in enchantments, Your Majesty?" her mother asked.

"I do not deny them. There are things in this world we cannot fully comprehend. However, if your daughter has indeed been enchanted, why come to me? I am no sorcerer."

"I understand, Your Majesty. You are my *king*. A mortal man. We stand here before you because there is someone in your care who is rumored to have the abilities. Until today, I did not accept that such things existed, but my daughter's *ailment* cannot be otherwise explained. I am led to believe that the particular aforementioned someone is vindictive—jealous of Alesa's abilities."

The king folded his hands over his stomach. "Of whom do you speak? This *aforementioned someone*?"

Her mother looked nervously from side to side. "The lady, Zeborah."

"I see." As before, he stroked his beard and did not seem at all astonished by the revelation. The man was handsome, but his smooth-faced brother surpassed him in appearance.

Alesa shut her eyes and shook her head, wondering what caused her mind to wander to something so trivial. She presently had more pertinent issues to ponder than which of the royal men she preferred to gaze at. Her interest likely had to do with being overly ripe for marriage. She had to stop fooling herself that it mattered not to her. For the past few years, she had found herself admiring men in general. Trouble was, *no one* would have her now…

"Have you nothing else to say, Your Majesty?" her mother persisted. "You do not seem surprised by my mention of her name."

Exactly!

"Sadly, I am not. Others have come to me in complaint with her name on their lips. My own brother—" King Lorin pinched off his words as if realizing he had spoken out of turn. Yet, a king could say whatever he pleased, so why correct himself? "That is another issue, not of your concern. Tell me, what made you conclude that Zeborah is the cause of your daughter's distress?

And what exactly is her ailment? My guard mentioned something about her voice."

"The reason, I feel, is jealousy. You proclaimed my Alesa to have the finest voice in the realm, and although Zeborah complimented her for it, we doubt her praise was genuine. We believe she came to our cottage in the dark hours of last night and cast a spell over Alesa. My sweet girl can no longer speak. When she tries, all she manages is song."

The king cocked his head and motioned Alesa even closer. "Let me hear you."

"Go on and show him," Farrah whispered and nudged Alesa's arm.

Alesa took a brave step toward King Lorin, cupped her hands together at her bosom, and pulled her shoulders back. "*A song is all I bear, to offer you, my king. Speaking is not there, but from my heart I sing.*"

He smiled. "My dear girl, you sang as lovely as you did in your performance for me. Why do you find this troublesome?"

"Is that a genuine question, Your Majesty?" her mother asked, wide-eyed, and Alesa rapidly nodded, needing an answer.

"Indeed, it is, Bithia. Your daughter has a gift many would envy. If this is an enchantment, I see it as a blessing."

"*No! It is not so!*" Alesa intently sang. "*It is a curse! Like nothing worse!*"

The king's head drew back. "Does she always rhyme with such melodic passion?"

Her mother frowned. "I am afraid so."

"May I speak?" Farrah said.

"You may." The king spun his hand in the air, encouraging her to continue.

"My sister most assuredly has a lovely voice. Even so, anything in excess can become annoying and no longer desirable. Will you be kind enough to ask Zeborah to remove this enchantment, so Alesa can resume a normal life?"

King Lorin studied them for several moments, looking from Farrah to their mother, then to Alesa, and back to Farrah again. "Guard!"

The man appeared out of nowhere. "Yes, Your Majesty?"

"Bring Lady Zeborah here."

"Yes, Your Majesty." The guard bowed and fled the room.

Alesa breathed easier, finally feeling a glimmer of hope, but almost immediately, she clenched up with fear once more.

Soon, she would be face to face with Zeborah.

Chapter 4

Denial

Zeborah paraded into the room, and a now-familiar icy chill permeated Alesa's body. Zeborah smiled in Alesa's direction—a disturbingly *large* one. Alesa detected a trace of ill-intended mischief in her jade-green eyes. Without a doubt, Zeborah enjoyed inflicting intimidation.

Farrah moved closer and slipped her hand back into Alesa's, and their mother hovered near as well. Zeborah passed by them, dusting Alesa's arm with the long, silky sleeve of her lavender gown. She approached the throne and bowed. "My king. You requested my presence?"

"I did indeed." He nervously licked his lips, which did not aid Alesa's confidence. If the king feared Zeborah, what hope did she have that he would help *her*?

Zeborah coyly tipped her head to one side. "How may I serve you?"

King Lorin cleared his throat. "Do you know the others here before me?" He gestured to the three of them.

Zeborah pivoted and faced them. "Hmm... I recall seeing them last night at the royal feast. Although I must say, they were dressed far better than they are now. That peasant..." She pointed at Alesa. "...sang for you." Zeborah's lips pursed. "*Beautifully*, I might add."

Alesa could easily vomit.

"*Quite* beautifully," the king interjected, and for the briefest instant, Zeborah's eyes opened wider, then returned to a normal state. "She has come before me in complaint of enchantment."

"Truly?" Zeborah covered her bosom, as if attempting to shield her heart. "How intriguing."

"In addition, she thinks *you* were somehow involved."

"*I?*" Zeborah released a light laugh. "How could I have been involved? I saw the girl for mere moments and have never touched her. What sort of spell is she under? *Delusion?*"

Farrah's grip tightened and the rate of her breathing increased. Alesa sensed her sister's intense anger, feeling just as much of her own. Yet, she kept her lips sealed, knowing it was for the best in many ways.

"Delusion?" Their mother hissed air from her nostrils and shook a stiff finger at Zeborah. "My daughter is sane and trustworthy! You, however—"

"Silence!" The king held up a hand. "You will speak only when I ask it of you."

Her mother's head lowered, and Alesa hurt for her. Her bold protectiveness had momentarily outweighed her good sense.

Zeborah briskly fanned herself. "Your interference is well received, Your Majesty. I feared I might be assaulted."

"I insist on order from *everyone*." King Lorin shifted his gaze from one of them to the next, driving his message. "Now then, Lady Zeborah, are you claiming no knowledge of this girl's enchantment?"

Zeborah opened her arms wide and shrugged. "I know not what could possibly be wrong with the dear girl." She turned toward Alesa. "She has the semblance of a perfectly normal peasant. Pray tell, what ails you?"

Alesa looked at the king in question.

"Go on," he said. "Reveal to her what you displayed to me."

As if it actually needed to be done. Alesa believed wholeheartedly that Zeborah had caused her troubles and was well aware that once she opened her mouth, she would sing. Still, she could not deny the king's request.

She mustered her courage and bravely faced Zeborah. "*I cannot speak a word, my voice will only sing. But unlike every bird, sheer torment this curse brings.*" Alesa fiercely stared at her as she sang and put great feeling into it. Maybe she could melt the woman's cold, jealous heart.

Zeborah grinned and applauded. "How marvelous! Am I to understand that you are enchanted to sing without end? Like the birds in the trees?"

"You know she is!" Farrah blurted out.

"Silence!" The king slapped the arm of his chair, while Zeborah cast a frightened expression and hastened nearer to his throne.

"And *you* cursed her, Zeborah!" Farrah raved on. "Just as you cursed Lady Ellen and the miller's wife! You are an evil witch!"

"Enough!" King Lorin shot to his feet and glared down at Farrah. "Another word and I will have you thrown from the castle!"

"Forgive her, Your Majesty," their mother begged. "She is an impassioned girl who dearly loves her sister and only wants to see the enchantment removed."

"That does not excuse such rude accusations. Did I not just make it clear that all present will only remark when asked to speak?" Breathing heavily, the king sat down again. "What proof do you have of Lady Zeborah's involvement in this sorcery?"

Alesa's mother regained her full composure and stood tall. "This morning, we found that the interior of our cottage had been dusted in a fine powder. Even our dog—who guards us—had it in his fur. It was blue in color. Almost purple. My daughter, Farrah, told me that a servant she knows saw a mist of the same color coming from beneath Lady Zeborah's door, and when he inhaled it, it made him light-headed. We feel we breathed in so much of it, it rendered us unconscious, enabling Zeborah to enter our home undetected and cast her spell on Alesa."

Zeborah watched Alesa's mother the entire time she spoke and acted mesmerized by the story.

"None of you actually *saw* Zeborah in your abode?" King Lorin asked.

"No, Your Majesty. We were in a deep slumber."

"And why do you believe that the powdery substance you discovered is the same as the mist you claim a servant witnessed?"

"The *color*, Your Majesty. It is quite unusual."

Zeborah laughed. "Do you not see the foolishness in this, my king? How can a mist become a powder, and how could I possibly be involved in any of this? I was in my chamber all night, thoroughly exhausted after having entertained your brother."

King Lorin cleared his throat.

"Oh." Zeborah's cheeks filled with a rosy blush. "I should make clear that I carried out none of my entertaining *in* my chamber. Only the sleep after, and I was most assuredly alone." She fluttered her lashes.

Farrah nudged Alesa with her elbow, and when Alesa looked at her, she rolled her eyes. Alesa felt just as much contempt for Zeborah, yet chose not to show it and put her full attention back on the king.

He shifted uneasily on his throne and faced Alesa. "From what I can discern, there is no evidence of Lady Zeborah's involvement in your enchantment. However, I do not deny that there is sorcery at play. If you seek answers and hope for relief from this spell, I suggest you seek out the alchemist, Waldemar."

Alesa moved her gaze to Zeborah whose eyes narrowed. As before, the woman's lips pursed, and she jutted her chin ever-so-slightly. Alesa shuddered. It felt as though she had silently said, *I put you in your place, little peasant.*

Her mother's eyes pooled with moisture. "May I speak, Your Majesty?"

He nodded.

"We will do as you have advised, yet I am not convinced of your ward's innocence. Take care, my king. A snake lurking in one's dwelling will bite when least expected." She bowed low.

"Your Majesty!" Zeborah defiantly protested. "If I am not mistaken, this woman just referred to me as a snake!"

"Enough, Zeborah. Lady Bithia has a right to her own opinions. They are mere words and cannot render harm."

"Lady? She is no *Lady*! She is a peasant and does not belong here."

"Guard!" The king waved him over, and Zeborah triumphantly beamed.

"Escort Lady Zeborah back to her chamber," King Lorin sternly demanded.

Zeborah stared at him in horror as the guard took her by the arm. "Yes, my king," he stoically said.

"*I* am to leave?" Zeborah shrieked. "I *belong* here! These peasants should be thrown in the dungeon for their accusations!"

King Lorin jerked his head, and the guard firmly guided Zeborah from the throne room. Her rants of disapproval rang out all the way down the long corridor.

Zeborah's voice finally fell silent after several long, uncomfortable moments.

The king heavily sighed. "I am not unwise or blind. I cannot act against Lady Zeborah without better proof, yet I am aware of her inclination to jealousy. I fear I have spoiled her to some degree, trying to repay my father's debt to her family."

He brought out a small cloth that he had tucked in his tunic and dabbed at his damp forehead. He looked directly at Farrah. "Even before today, rumors came to my ears of her connection to the miller's wife *and* Lady Ellen. I assure you, Zeborah is being closely watched. If I discover she is indeed practicing sorcery, she will be banished from Shanavar."

Farrah circled her finger with a lock of hair. "It pleases me to hear it, Your Majesty."

Their mother wiped her tears. "But what of Alesa? She is suffering because of Zeborah. Banishing her from the kingdom will not change the harm that has already been done."

The king frowned. "It pains me that sorcery is at play in my realm—no matter who rendered it. Go to Waldemar. He is a good man and exceedingly wise. As for Zeborah's involvement, if I discover that she casts enchantments, I am certain she would not undo them. She has claimed innocence, and I know her well. She would never admit to telling falsehoods."

Farrah sniffled. "It is so unfair."

King Lorin slowly nodded. "I am inclined to agree with you, young one, but there are many unfair experiences in life." He gave Farrah a sad, slim smile, then turned to Alesa and offered her a much brighter one. "When you sang for me, your words came from your heart. I advise you to make the best of your circumstances. Your voice is a gift, and used properly, you could soothe many souls."

Alesa wanted to respond, but at present, she did not care to sing. Her hopes had been utterly diminished. She had heard alchemists were known to dabble in sorcery—to a different degree. Supposedly, they used their talents for good, not evil.

Certainly, *he* had not cast the enchantment over her, so she feared he would not be able to undo it. How could he help her at all?

In spite of her misgivings, the king's kind remarks touched a small corner of her heart, though it horribly ached, making it difficult to appreciate what he had said. In time, perhaps, she could fully embrace it.

"Thank you, Your Majesty." Fortunately, Alesa's mother voiced what she could not. "We will go to the alchemist."

King Lorin got to his feet. "Very well. I will escort you to the gate."

"Your Majesty?" Her mother gaped at him, and Alesa understood why. It was not the king's place to escort lowly peasants *anywhere*.

He stepped down from the platform. "I wish I could aid you more. At least, taking you to the gate is something I *can* do." He fanned his arm toward the hallway and headed in that direction.

They hurriedly followed. Alesa had grown up being taught to have loyalty to her king, but his gracious actions brought out a new respect for the man.

The courtyard soon became a flurry of whispers from the strolling ladies to the guards, and anyone else they passed. Her mother walked even prouder as they exited through the gate. It shut soundly behind them again.

Alesa glanced back at the tall barrier.

Will we ever be granted reentry? And do I desire it? It favorably struck her that her thoughts were free from rhyme. A blessing she embraced.

They walked some distance, and neither Farrah nor their mother spoke. Alesa had already become fairly used to the idea of keeping *her* mouth sealed, and not talking opened up another world for her. She heard more than ever. The birds seemed to sing with greater sweetness, and the water in the distant brook pleasantly trickled with a melody of its own. A bee buzzed in the nearby wildflowers, and she startled when a fly zipped by her head and tickled her ears with the rapid sound it made.

"For a moment," Farrah whispered, breaking nature's spell, "I feared the king was a hateful man. I am happy to know he is kind."

"Yes, he is a good man," their mother said. "As well as a *king*. I believe he behaved as he did because he had to show strength in front of Zeborah. In addition, he had the right to chastise you for speaking out of turn in such a scornful manner, just as he did to me. I suppose we must learn to hold our tongues, Farrah. The king deserves our respect, even though we were both angered."

"*As was I.*" Alesa quickly covered her mouth, having briefly forgotten her impairment. She did *not* want to rhyme, especially with something so serious.

Regardless of her beautiful surroundings, self-pity overtook her, and she silently allowed her tears to stream.

Chapter 5

The Alchemist

"Oh, my…" Farrah bent down just inside their cottage doorway and ruffled Bo's fur. "You are still covered in powder. I thought by now you would have shaken it all off."

Alesa closely eyed the dog and hoped the substance did not have any lasting effects. "*He must be bathed, so he is not scathed,*" she keenly sang.

Farrah peered up at her and nodded.

Their mother bustled past them and entered the cottage. "Farrah, take Bo to the creek and bathe him, while I start sweeping the floors. Once I have cleaned our home properly, I will make soup. I want you both to eat a decent meal and try to get a good night's rest. On the morrow, we will go to the alchemist."

"Yes, Mother." Farrah lightly touched her arm. "May Alesa accompany me to the creek?"

"I could use her help here." She glanced at Alesa with the saddest eyes. "However, it might do her well to be away from this mess."

"Thank you, Mother." Farrah spun and faced Alesa, grinning.

Did her sister have ulterior motives?

Whatever her reason, Alesa liked the idea of being removed from the reminders of how she became enchanted. She crossed to their mother and kissed her cheek.

The dear woman gingerly fingered the damp spot. "What was that for?"

"*I am proud to be your daughter and appreciate your care. You stood up to Zeborah in matters so unfair. You set a bold example to Farrah and to me. I hope to be as strong, accepting all that comes to be.*"

"Oh, my sweet girl." Her mother embraced her. "I would do anything for you." She pulled back and framed Alesa's face with her hands. "King Lorin did not lie. Your voice is a blessed gift, and I am grateful Zeborah did not alter it to sound grating and poor. This curse could be far worse."

"Yes," Farrah rapidly added. "She could have been made *mute*. That was my fear."

Their mother looked from Farrah to Alesa and smiled with so much love, it melted away some of the pain from Alesa's heart. "Go on and see to Bo." She kissed them both on their foreheads, then retrieved the broom and set to sweeping.

Farrah circled Bo's neck with the rope they used to keep him from running off, and Alesa headed off with them toward the creek. Bo hated the water and bathing him was always a chore. Fortunately, they had plenty of daylight left to complete their task. The sun brightly beamed down upon them.

They passed row after row of thatch-roofed cottages, and several villagers out working in their gardens looked at them strangely.

Farrah giggled. "I suppose a blue dog justifies their inquisitive gazes."

Bo happily trotted along—no doubt unaware of his unusual appearance or upcoming bath—and bits of colorful powder floated onto the road. It had deeply embedded itself into his thick, white fur. Zeborah must have put additional amounts of the odd substance on him to keep him slumbering. Thankfully, it had not killed him. Alesa's heart would have broken if she lost the last thing gifted to her and Farrah by their father.

They neared the bank of the creek, and Bo froze in his tracks. He sat on his rump and blinked up at Farrah, whining.

"You cannot stay this color forever, silly dog." She tugged on the rope, but Bo would not budge.

Alesa crossed to him and scooped him into her arms, disregarding the dusting of color he transferred onto her dress. *"Fear not, sweet Bo, we will make this quick. If only your fur were not so thick."*

Farrah unfastened her boots, took them off, and laid them on the grassy embankment. She stepped into the water, grinning even more broadly than before. "Pass him to me."

Alesa gladly obliged. The dog was by no means small, yet Farrah had no trouble managing him and did not seem to mind getting herself wet. She set the dog in the water, kept a tight grip on the rope, and briskly rubbed through his fur with her free hand. Purple-blue rivulets flowed off him and washed downstream.

Bo slowly returned to his original color: creamy white.

Farrah brought him out of the water, and he vigorously shook. Alesa had the good sense to jump out of range before he showered her with his spray. After several hefty shakes, he stood on the edge of the creek, wagging his tail.

"We should sit for a moment." Farrah gestured to a particularly grassy spot.

Alesa liked the idea. Not only did it give them more time away from the assaulted cottage, but she also hoped her sister would reveal what lay behind her grins and the reason she requested that she accompany her.

Alesa tucked her dress under her bottom and lowered herself to the ground. She tipped her head back and breathed in the sweet-scented air. Honeysuckles bloomed from a large, nearby vine, and they emitted the incredible aroma.

Bare-footed, Farrah sat beside her, along with Bo. He curled up next to Farrah, getting her even wetter. "I am thankful the day is warm. Perhaps we will be dry once we decide to go home."

"*We should not tarry long.*" Alesa dramatically shook a finger at her sister. "*It would be very wrong.*"

"Why? Because Mother is cleaning the cottage without us?"

Alesa nodded.

"But I know you wanted to leave, and Mother encouraged you to go. So, do not feel bad about lingering here awhile. In addition, we need to talk."

Alesa sighed, widened her eyes, and rubbed her throat.

"I know you cannot actually *talk*, but I have to tell you something. A conclusion I have come to."

Alesa circled her hand, encouraging her to continue.

"King Lorin was right about you—just as Mother said. It must be awful wanting to simply talk, and I was horribly angry with Zeborah for doing this to you. But when I think about what happened to Lady Ellen—her painfully broken bones—I feel you were spared true torment. And although there is no pain involved in losing one's hair, the miller's wife is shamed by her appearance.

There is nothing shameful or painful in *your* enchantment. If you indeed have to permanently live with this, could you not *try* to view it as a gift?"

Alesa drew her knees to her chest, leaned against them, and peered at the sparkling creek. A tear trickled down her cheek. How could she embrace what she did not desire?

"It hurts me to see you cry." Farrah lightly rubbed her back. "I know you well, and I can tell you are purposefully not speaking. Please share your thoughts. I *want* to hear you sing."

A bird chirped overhead, knowing nothing but song. Could *she* adapt to such a way of living?

She sat fully upright and faced her sister. "*It is not my voice that saddens me, or the songs that I must sing. But the freedom taken from me for the way my words I bring.*"

Farrah's brows wove with concern. "I think I understand." She pushed out a smile. "It is remarkable how you so ably rhyme."

"*Dear sister you are charming, and I hope you never change.*" Alesa glanced around them, wondering if anyone was nearby. "*But will I soon become a spectacle and have our lives rearranged?*"

"You fear what the villagers will say once they learn you are enchanted?"

Alesa frowned. "*I fear their endless teasing and their lack of empathy. I may be a pariah who no one wants to see.*"

Farrah shook her head. "I believe it will be quite the opposite. They will want to hear you sing, just as I do." She peered deeply into Alesa's eyes. "Let us cast aside our worries until we speak with the alchemist and discover whether or not he can cure you."

Or, he could possibly ruin her voice forever, by giving her some kind of untested concoction. The man was said to be constantly mixing formulas and remedies for ailments, but he was also very old, and aged people oftentimes lost their sensibility. Could he be trusted to have retained his?

Alesa pushed off the ground and stood. "*Mother may need us, we should go. Put on your boots and do not tarry so.*"

Farrah did as she requested and yanked on her boots. "Are you angry with me?"

"*Angry*?" She sealed her lips. The one word certainly did not need a rhyming counterpart.

"Yes. Because I suggested that your enchantment might not be a bad thing."

Alesa pulled her still-damp sister into a hug. "*Looking at the bright side is never bad, dear girl. My frustration is confusion and it keeps my thoughts awhirl.*"

Farrah tightly squeezed her, then released her, giggling. "Girl is not an easy word to rhyme. As I said before, your gift is truly remarkable."

Was it indeed?

Alesa had yet to be convinced. At present, she found it an annoying intrusion and a violation of her freedom. She became a performing puppet whenever she opened her mouth. How could that be a gift?

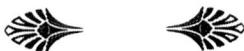

A mist-like rain fell, making the trek to the alchemist's cottage less appealing than their journey to the castle. At least it was not a downpour.

Unfortunately, the man lived on the opposite end of Shanavar, and being the largest realm in the land, it took Alesa, Farrah, and their mother half a day's walk to get there.

"I wish we had traveled yesterday," Farrah fussed. "The weather was more accommodating."

"How could we have known?" Their mother headed for a small cottage with a green door. "This is the one." She pointed at a curious symbol painted at the door's center—a circle with a triangle, square, and another circle within it.

Alesa's insides fluttered. Soon, she would be in the presence of someone who believed in things far beyond her comprehension. Was he genuinely wise or a doddering old fool?

Her mother rapped soundly on the door.

Alesa's loving companions looked worse for the wear, and she assumed she appeared no better. Her long, blond hair lay matted against her head and clothes, and mud had spattered up onto the base of her dress from their brisk walking.

We will make a wonderful first impression.

No one answered, so her mother knocked louder.

Finally, the door swung open. "For the sake of heaven, give an old man time to answer before battering my door." Waldemar stood hunched over in his grayish-white robe, and his long, fully white beard nearly touched his knees.

"Forgive me, sir," her mother kindly said. "We have come to you by recommendation from the king."

Waldemar grunted. "I see. Well. Come in out of the rain and warm yourselves by the fire." He cautiously eyed each of them and opened his door wider to allow them entry.

Her mother bravely went in first, followed by Farrah. Alesa tentatively stepped across the threshold. An odd smell permeated the interior of the place—both bitter and sweet. *Strange, to say the least.*

Alesa took everything in, and there was much to see. Shelves filled with jars, bones, and metal trinkets lined the walls. Tapestries hung behind them with similar symbols sewn into their design as was on the front door. Surely, they all had meaning, and it piqued Alesa's curiosity.

She startled, almost tripping over a cat. Strangely, it did not move, and after a quick study of the thing, she determined it to be mummified. Other dead animals—squirrels, rabbits, and even a small dog—were randomly scattered here and there, and she shuddered. If not for the king's referral, she would have turned and fled.

The cluttered interior barely gave them a path to the fireplace. Her mother continued to lead the way, and she and Farrah closely followed. Once there, Alesa put her back to the flames, and a man sitting bent over at a desk in the far corner caught her eye. He paid them no mind whatsoever. He faced away from them and seemed to be intently working on something, yet his body blocked her view. With all the dead creatures lying about, she honestly did not want to know what he might be doing.

So many oddities.

Waldemar shuffled across the floor. He groaned as he eased down into an overstuffed chair near the fire. His knees popped so loud; the sound surpassed his groans. "What brings you?"

"My daughter, Alesa," her mother said. "She has been enchanted, and King Lorin thought you may be able to help."

Like before, the man grunted. "I am no sorcerer."

"But you are," Farrah interjected. "You are an alchemist, and from my understanding, you do magic."

"Magic?" He scowled and waved a hand. "Bah! I work with all that is natural in this world. I am a learned man who grasps the complex properties of every element, and I seek the means to transform them. I have mastered many feats."

"Can you transform my sister? Make her more *natural* again?"

The old man's eyes pinched into slits, and he keenly studied Alesa. "You are the one of whom she refers?"

Alesa nodded, and all the while her insides quaked.

"You already appear to be quite natural." He wiggled his finger at her. "Soaked and earthy."

"She is unable to speak," her mother said. "She can only sing."

The man's head drew back, and a low chuckle emerged from deep within him. "It seems Zeborah's creativity has blossomed."

"You know of her?"

"Of course. She is the only one I have been apprised of in Shanavar who dabbles in sorcery, and I have had previous visitors come before me seeking relief from her practices. I cannot undo what she has done, nor can I comprehend why King Lorin continues to send people asking for my aid. He should dismiss his feelings of loyalty to his father—in her regard—and banish her. Truthfully, it should have been done when he first heard of her experimentations. He would have been finished with her, and others—such as yourself—would not have been harmed."

Alesa's dreaded tears returned. His words affirmed that their assumptions about Zeborah were well-founded, and as she had assumed, there was no hope for her.

Waldemar lifted his head high. "Why are you crying, young one?"

"*You laughed at my pain, and I prayed you were good. There is no help to gain, as I feared that it would.*" She rubbed her aching throat. Between the pain from her tears, the cold, and endless singing, she could get no relief.

Waldemar folded his old, gnarled hands on his lap and leaned forward. "You must forgive my laughter. It was not directed at your pain, my dear, but at Zeborah's unique dabbling. My ears have never enjoyed such a pure and rich voice, and I cannot perceive why Zeborah would gift you with something so lovely. There is no reason to it."

"Her voice has always been beautiful," her mother whispered. "The enchantment did nothing to alter it. Yet, Alesa cannot speak or carry on a normal conversation. You can certainly understand how troubling that is."

"Hmm." He tapped his chin and put his focus on Alesa once more. "I see how you rub your throat. Does it hurt to sing?"

She simply nodded again, not wanting to voice another thought.

"Well, that I *can* help." Waldemar pivoted in his chair, dug into his pocket, and withdrew a small object. He pinched it between his fingers, then threw it at the man in the corner. Whatever it was struck him in the head.

The man's shoulders lurched. He jumped to his feet, spun around, and faced them. His eyes opened as wide as saucers, as if stunned by their presence in the room.

Alesa's insides quivered for a very different reason. The man was young and exceedingly handsome. Like Prince Chadwick, he had no facial hair, just smooth, perfectly formed features and the curliest brown hair she had ever seen. His kind eyes met hers, and he smiled.

Why had he not reacted to them before now, and why did Waldemar throw something at him to gain his attention?

He hastened across the floor and stood before the alchemist.

Waldemar lifted a teacup from a table beside him, handed it to the young man, and pointed at her. He then rubbed his throat and grimaced as if hurting.

The young man rapidly bobbed his head and bustled off.

"That was Pim," Waldemar said. "My assistant. He cannot hear, nor can he speak. Thus, he is the perfect aide for me. When I make my discoveries, I have no fear that my secrets will be revealed."

"What did you throw at him?" Farrah asked.

"A dried bean." Waldemar withdrew another one from his pocket and showed it to them. "I assure you, they do not render him harm. I keep them readily available. Consider me lazy, but once I sit, I prefer to stay seated, and I needed a means to gain his attention. Clever, is it not?"

"I suppose so, but how does he know what you want?" Farrah persisted.

"He came into my employ as a boy of seven, and we have learned to understand one another over the years through gestures. I had hoped to teach him to read. As of yet, he has not grasped the concept."

Pim returned with the cup and motioned toward the fireplace.

"He needs you to step aside," Waldemar said, "so he can reach the pot of water."

They parted for him.

Pim glanced at Alesa as he passed by, fluttering her insides again. This close, he looked even finer.

He grabbed a rag lying on the crudely cut mantel and used it to remove the lid from the pot that dangled from a wrought-iron hanger above the fire. He ladled steaming water into the cup, stirred its contents with a spoon, sniffed it, and extended it to Alesa. She took it, and he held up his hands in a cautionary motion.

"He is telling you to drink carefully because it is hot," Waldemar said.

"*What is in the cup? It smells quite sweet and tasty. Should I drink it up, or sip and not be hasty?*"

Pim watched her—brows weaving—as if wanting to understand her words, and Waldemar released a much heftier chuckle. "Forgive me, young one. Your rhyme humored me."

She huffed, tipped her head, and repeated the question with her eyes while pointing a rigid finger at the teacup.

Waldemar grinned. "It appears *you* have a gift for gestures as well. The cup holds tea with honey, made from a special blend of herbs that will soothe your throat. If you look in the cup you will see a small cloth bag—an idea I invented. Rather than pouring the hot water over the herbs and through a strainer, I enclose them in cloth and tie the ends with twine to keep the tiny particles from escaping. The longer the water steeps the tea, the stronger it will be. Since it is hot, I suggest you sip it."

She glanced at her mother who gave an encouraging dip of her head.

Alesa stared into the cup. It did indeed have a small bag within it. From the enticing aroma, she deemed it safe and took a sip. The sweetness of the honey pleased her, and the warmth alone from the tea aided her throat.

Pim continued watching her with his caring eyes. How sad that he could not hear or speak. Knowing *his* condition, hers did not seem so troublesome.

She pointed into the cup, then rubbed her throat again—this time with a large smile directed right at Pim. She also sipped a bit more to make sure he understood that she found the beverage favorable.

He beamed and pulled his shoulders back, straightening himself fully tall.

Waldemar chortled in a different manner. "He likes you. Rarely does anyone bother attempting any sort of communication with him."

"That is quite sad," Farrah said. "He must be terribly lonely."

"He has *me*." Waldemar lifted a single brow. "I may not be as pleasant to look at, but I keep him busy and fed." He waved in front of Pim, and Pim's gaze locked onto him.

Waldemar pointed at Alesa's teacup, then fanned his hands wide. He followed that gesture by walking two of his long fingers along the back of his other hand, and ended by jerking his chin in the direction of the door.

Pim's shoulders slumped. He frowned and trudged off.

Alesa's heart sank. It pained her to see him looking so defeated.

"What did you tell him?" Fortunately, her mother asked the very thing she had wondered.

"I told him you would be going and to get more tea for you to take with you."

His gestures made sense, and Alesa assumed after years of living and working side by side, it had become less complicated for the two men to communicate.

Her mother's face drew up with concern. "So, we are to leave now?"

"What reason is there for you to linger? I cannot help your daughter in any other way."

"But…" Her mother rubbed across her heart. "Is there nothing—"

"She is enchanted. No one other than Zeborah can undo what has been done." Waldemar reached for Alesa's hand, and she hesitantly took hold. "Be grateful for your voice, young one." He patted her hand with his bony fingers and released her.

Her mother sniffled and opened the satchel that dangled from her wrist. She withdrew a coin and held it out for the alchemist. "For your time, sir, and the tea, of course."

He shook his head. "I do not want your money, yet it was kind of you to offer. Normally, I am presented with chickens or eggs."

"Are you certain? I did not expect your services to be without pay."

"Keep your money, dear lady. I do my best to stay aware of those residing in Shanavar, and if I am not mistaken, you are widowed. Coins are not easily attained by those of your stature."

Alesa earnestly watched their interchange. Her mother had taken that coin from the funds they used to buy meat. The man was right. The meager money they earned from doing laundry and mending did not last long and was a rarity. Most people tended their own clothing.

Her mother securely tucked the coin back into her satchel.

Pim returned, walked toward Alesa, and held out a cloth bag. She took it from him, and their hands touched for the briefest moment. They both gasped. A surprising spark had tickled her skin, and from his astonished expression, she believed he also felt it. Was this some other sort of magic?

She let out an uncomfortable laugh, relieved he could not hear it. Her heart did a series of unexpected flips deep within her chest. She needed to put her thoughts elsewhere, so she peered into the bag and counted five, tied smaller bags within it. Surely, they contained the blended herbs.

She turned to the alchemist. "*I thank you for your kindness and this gracious, soothing tea. And for the time you made to see my family and me.*"

Waldemar respectfully nodded. "You are quite welcome. Pim will show you out." He gestured at Pim, then at them, and then to the door.

Pim fanned his arm and headed that way, frowning. Without a doubt, he did not want them to go, and as concerned as she had been in coming there, oddly, she wanted to stay. Still, they dutifully followed him.

He opened the door to a waft of chilled air that seemed to have come from nowhere—as if it had blown down from the high peaks of Mount Ashalon. A torrent of rain accompanied it.

Pim spun around and widened both his eyes *and* his arms, staring at his master.

"Oh, bother." Waldemar groaned, painstakingly rose to his feet, and shuffled toward them. "You are likely to catch your death if you travel back to your home in this storm. Gretchen will give you lodging for the night."

Alesa's mother cocked her head. "Gretchen?"

"The proprietor of the tavern a short distance up the road. Are you not familiar with it?"

"No, sir. We do not patronize such establishments."

Waldemar grunted. "For the night, I suggest you do. You will easily find it. It is marked by a sign depicting a tankard of ale. You can request a bed *without ale* and use the coin you offered me to pay for it. It should also afford you an acceptable meal."

Her mother sharply nodded. "Very well. Come, girls."

Since they would not be returning home, it was good they had asked someone to tend Bo while they were gone. Nothing was transpiring as Alesa had hoped, and their night would not be anything like she had assumed it would be. Then again, her entire life had become a series of the unexpected.

Chapter 6

A Crying Babe

Boisterous laughter filtered from the tavern. The sign over the door had not been needed to find it, since the large structure stood out from the simple cottages lining the road. The sound alone coming from the place gave it away, and Alesa believed many inebriated patrons filled it. She feared staying there would be unwise and exchanged worried looks with both her mother and sister.

Her mother stared at the closed door. "We have little choice but to enter." The rain fell so hard it bounced off her lips as she spoke. She took a large breath and opened the door.

Alesa peered at the upper floor of the establishment before going inside. Shuttered windows lined the outer walls, and presumably, the guestrooms were on that level.

Many heads snapped in their direction as they entered, yet every gaze was short-lived. The men resumed their raucous drinking with excessively loud conversation.

"You poor dears!" A sprightly, red-haired woman rushed toward them. "You are soaked to the bone. Come." She waved for them to follow.

Alesa's mother motioned to her and Farrah. "We will do as she says, girls."

"I am Gretchen," the woman said over her shoulder as they walked. "This is my establishment. I call it The Keep. I assume you have come for a room?" She stopped at a long bar, went behind it, and brought out several towels. She gave one to each of them, and they eagerly dried their faces and hands.

"Thank you." Alesa's mother briskly rubbed the towel along her arms. "We do require lodging—and perhaps something to eat?"

"Will pottage suffice? It is seasoned well and will warm your insides."

"You cheated!" a man screamed from the other side of the room.

"How dare you accuse me!" another man countered.

"Excuse me for a moment." Gretchen brusquely nodded and bustled off. She paraded across the floor and put herself between the two men. One of them had a chair raised high above him and appeared to be ready to strike with it.

"You know the rules!" Gretchen fumed. "You may drink, laugh as powerfully as you desire, and even gamble, but if you fight, you will leave and never be allowed to return!" Leering, she spun and faced the man wielding the chair. "Break one piece of my furnishings, and you will be indebted to me for a sum greater than that of a wooden seat."

The man sheepishly lowered it to the floor.

"A wise decision!" Her gaze shifted between the two men. "If you have something to settle, do it outside. Otherwise, consider your differences resolved. I suggest you stop throwing dice and drink more ale."

The men scowled but almost immediately grinned.

"Barkeep!" one of them bellowed. "More ale!"

They patted each other on the back and headed for the bar. Alesa's mother scooted her and Farrah farther away to the very end of it.

Gretchen crossed over to them and stood beside Farrah. "Men can be beasts. However, I know how to tame them. Food and drink are all they need."

"And the love of a fine woman!" one of them shouted.

Gretchen rolled her eyes and leaned close to Alesa's mother. "I assure you, it will not be me. The barkeep is my husband, and they are well aware of it."

"Now I understand why you can be so bold. Your husband can defend you should the need arise."

Gretchen laughed. "*I* am the one they fear. I wield a wicked broom when necessary and sweep belligerent patrons out the door."

Farrah giggled. "I would like to see that."

"Sweet girl." Gretchen smoothed a hand down Farrah's damp hair. "You are too young to be witnessing any of this. My hope is that as the night wanes, the men will calm, and all of us can have some peace. Go and have a seat at the board near the fire. I will fill your bellies with pottage, then show you to a room." She worked her lower lip with her teeth. "Have you coins to pay?"

Alesa's mother once again dug the single coin from her satchel. "Will this be enough for food *and* beds?"

Gretchen snatched it from her. "Indeed. I will bring three bowls." She shooed them off toward the fire.

They took seats at the *board.* The entire establishment had no ordinary tables. The wooden eating surfaces consisted of long planks that sat atop empty ale barrels. It seemed reasonable—especially if some of the patrons were known to break furniture. Fancy tables would be costlier to replace.

The door opened and more travelers entered. As before, the activity in the place briefly halted before resuming to a loud roar.

Gretchen brought over three bowls of steaming pottage, hurriedly set them on the board, and bustled away to the newcomers.

Alesa sniffed the contents of her bowl. It smelled better than the tavern itself, which reeked of ale, manure—likely brought in from the men's boots—and the unpleasant scent of overly sweaty bodies. Did all alehouses smell this way? Aside from the intriguing adventure Alesa found herself in the midst of, she had no intention of repeating it.

Ever.

Farrah spooned up a bite of the stew and warily tasted it. "Hmm. It is not as good as yours, Mother, but I can eat it."

Their mother smiled and sampled her own. "It is better than nothing."

Alesa went ahead and took a bite, and as she did so, she recognized one of the people who had come in.

Pim.

His eyes locked with hers, and her heart flipped.

She elbowed Farrah, then jerked her chin in Pim's direction.

"I wonder why *he* is here," Farrah said. "Do you suppose he is fond of ale?"

Their mother looked his way. "Perhaps he merely came to make certain we got settled."

Pim sat near the door, some distance from them. At present, he had no beverage, and Alesa believed it unlikely that he had come to drink.

"He is fortunate to not be bothered by the sounds," Farrah said. "I can scarcely hear my own thoughts."

A baby wailed, and the shrill sound carried above all others.

"A babe?" Alesa's mother craned her neck. "The child came with the newcomers. They appear to be husband and wife."

Alesa turned to better see them. They, too, had gotten caught in the downpour. The rain had drenched the couple through and through and even soaked the blanket the baby had been wrapped in.

Gretchen gave them towels, just as she had done for them. Yet, even when the child's mother tried to dry and warm it, its cries did not lessen. She carried the infant in front of the fire, bounced the baby up and down, and cooed to it, but the little one did not calm. Its wails intensified.

"Shut the brat up!" a full-bearded man cried out from where he sat drinking with three other men.

The infant's mother's eyes pooled with tears, and she beseechingly looked toward her husband. He sat at one of the long boards, clutching a cup of wine Gretchen had brought him. Wine cost a great deal more than ale, making it an outward indication of the man's wealth. Surely, he was high in stature.

The man with the thick beard stood and stepped closer to the woman and baby. "Did you not hear me?" His words sounded slightly slurred. "Quiet that child, or I will toss it out into the rain!"

Fast as a strike of lightning, the baby's father removed his cape, shot to his feet, and wielded a gleaming sword. "Touch my child and you will find yourself without a hand!" He rigidly widened his stance, mere feet from the other man.

The raised voice of the baby's father made it cry harder. Something Alesa did not think possible. For such a tiny thing it had remarkable volume.

"Saints help us," Gretchen mumbled and once again put herself in the middle of the fray. Her disposition this time seemed much less self-assured. The shining sword hovered above her head. "We must have calm."

"Calm?" the bearded man hissed through his teeth. "I fear no sword from this *coxcomb*!" Without a doubt, the ale had emboldened him. He fumbled around at his ankle and pulled a long knife from a strap on his boot.

Alesa glanced at Pim, who gazed fearfully at the scene. Although he could not hear, he obviously sensed and *saw* the rising anger. The brandished sword and knife said plenty.

A desire to do something—*anything* to keep the situation from escalating—flooded over her, and she hastened to Gretchen's side.

"Alesa, what are you doing?" Farrah shrieked, but she ignored her.

She held out her hands to the baby's mother, offering her aid. Every eye rested on her, yet she did not care. At least, the fracas had momentarily stopped.

The woman fearfully looked about. "You want to help my baby boy?"

Alesa certainly hoped she could and bravely nodded.

The woman tentatively passed the screaming child into Alesa's arms. Perhaps the magnifying situation prompted her to trust a stranger. A towel had been wrapped around the baby, but the chill of the boy's body permeated it. He squirmed and cried so hard, he gasped for air between each outburst, and his face turned a brilliant shade of red.

Alesa held him close and swayed. "*Precious baby, do not cry. I will lull you by and by. Listen to the words I sing. Peace to you I bring.*" The babe sucked in several breaths and stopped crying altogether. She placed a tender kiss on his forehead. "*Peace to you, I bring.*"

She repeated the entire song, and a deathly quiet fell throughout the tavern. The child's father sheathed his weapon, and the bearded man bent down, teetered, and felt around his ankle until he managed to get his knife back into its place.

Alesa smiled at the baby boy as she sang the last line, and he peered up at her and silently blinked several times.

"Here, here!" the bearded man hollered, then belched. "Sing it again!"

Alesa gladly did as he requested. When she finished, applause erupted.

The noise startled the baby, and he fussed, but nowhere near the loudness of his screeching wails. She sang softly—just for him—and he completely calmed once more.

Alesa gently gave him back to his mother.

"We cannot thank you enough," the boy's father said. "I am Sir Jonas. My wife is Ida, and my son is Jace. I believe I heard your mother call you *Alesa*?"

She nodded.

Her voiceless response brought looks of confusion from both Ida and Sir Jonas. If only she could answer them with unmelodic simplicity. She guided them over to her mother and Farrah, needing them to assist with communication.

Her mother stood. "I feared for my daughter when she put herself in danger, and I am grateful no blood was shed. My daughter is gifted with her voice, is she not?"

"Indeed," Sir Jonas said. "On most occasions, my son is not so easily calmed." The knight faced Alesa. "How did you become so gifted with *children*?"

"Her voice has always brought calm," her mother said. "To young and old alike."

Sir Jonas grunted. "Do you make a habit of speaking for your daughter?"

"She cannot speak for herself," Farrah interjected from her seat at the long board. "She has been enchanted and can only sing."

Ida's eyes widened, and she stepped back, clutching the baby tighter.

"Do not be afraid," Farrah went on. "My sister is good. I cannot say the same for the evil sorceress who bewitched her."

"Might it be Zeborah?" Sir Jonas knowingly asked.

Alesa's mother stared at him. "You are aware of her activities?"

"Yes. I was recently commissioned to watch over her, but I feared her and what she would do to my wife or our child if I crossed her." The brave man lowered his head. "I am ashamed to say that I fled from the castle with my family." Slowly, he lifted his chin high again. "My brief time away reminded me of my duty to the realm, and we were on our way back to King Lorin when we became caught in the downpour. We came into the tavern only because I wanted to drown my shame with wine."

"Will you be punished?" Farrah earnestly asked.

"It is possible. However, King Lorin has always been fair-minded. I hope he will understand the concern I had for my family's safety." He smiled at his wife. She returned his loving expression and swayed with baby Jace, now sleeping in her arms.

Sir Jonas faced Alesa again. "Your voice is not cursed. It is blessed." He lightly chortled. "Might I employ you to soothe my son whenever needed?"

Farrah peered up at him. "You would pay her to sing?"

"Indeed."

Gretchen bustled over to them with three tankards and soundly set them on the board. "The men are asking for another song. They told me to bring you drink—though I doubt you want it—and they also said to give you this." She displayed a gold coin and held it aloft in front of Alesa. "My patrons can manage loud talk, laughter, cursing, and screams, but the shriek of a baby puts them on edge. It does little for me as well. Will you honor us with another song?"

Alesa gaped at the coin. It alone would buy them meat for many months. Her hand shook as she reached out to take it. "*I will gladly sing for the joy I bring.*"

"And the money," Farrah added with a grin.

Gretchen laughed. "Just give us a song less soothing. Can you accomplish a *lively* tune?"

Alesa firmly clasped the coin in her fist. For a sum like that, she would sing *whatever* they wanted. She sauntered to the center of the room.

"Hoist her high!" someone yelled, and before she even blinked, numerous hands grabbed onto her and lifted her atop the bar.

She slightly wavered, but steadied herself and smoothed her mud-splattered dress. Needing a bolster of encouragement, she glanced at her mother and sister. Her mother appeared less enthusiastic than Farrah who seemed utterly enthralled with the experience and vigorously clapped. Alesa shifted her gaze to Pim.

He looked as wary as her mother, but his eyes sparkled when they met hers. He gave her a nod and circled his hand.

He assuredly wanted her to proceed.

She had no need to worry. The enchantment had proved that when she opened her mouth, the appropriate words would come forth.

"*Good patrons drink your ale! You are looking rather pale! A draft or two will bring, some color as I sing!*" *My heavens…*She found herself practically strutting atop the bar.

The men hooted and hollered.

"*Lift your mugs up high! Let out a gleeful cry! When you require more, Gretchen will merrily pour!*"

Gretchen shook a fist in the air, grinning. "Here, here!"

Alesa repeated the song, and by the third time she sang it, the others in the tavern joined in, jubilantly singing. She ended the tune, and the men applauded and placed additional coins on the bar at her feet.

Exhausted, Alesa fanned her face, and the men called for Gretchen to bring more ale.

Pim crossed to Alesa, cast a large smile, and held up a hand. Something about him tugged deeper at her heart than anything she had ever felt before. She carefully sat, then allowed him to help her off the bar. Although she wanted to give him her full attention, she made sure to gather all the coins. Never had she imagined that her songs would bring such joy or money.

Pim pointed at her, then up at the bar. He followed that by rubbing his hand over his heart and smiling as broadly as before.

She *thought* she understood. Was he saying he liked what she did? With the inability to hear, how could he fully appreciate her performance? She tipped her head and questioned with her eyes.

He gazed upward as if trying to figure out how to convey his answer, then gestured around the room at everyone there. Dreamily smiling, he crossed both arms over his chest as if hugging himself and swayed back and forth.

She rapidly nodded, motioned around as he had done, laid a hand to her heart, and smiled, then pointed at her open mouth and splayed her fingers out as though the words were bursting from it. Would he know that she meant to say, *they loved my voice*?

He nodded with greater enthusiasm than she had.

They stared at each other.

How much more could be said in silence?

Her mother touched her shoulder, startling her from her thoughts. "We need to go to our room and get some rest. We have had enough excitement for one night."

Alesa reluctantly dipped her head in acknowledgment and put her full attention on Pim again. She placed a flat palm to her heart, then gestured to her mother and sister. Lastly, she pressed her hands together as in prayer, leaned her cheek against them, and shut her eyes. When she reopened them, she found Pim nodding his understanding.

He pointed at the door, bowed, and walked away.

She sighed as he left. Her heart wrenched from the simple idea of him leaving. It took substantial effort to communicate with him, but something told her that Pim was well worth it.

Jeanne Hardt

Chapter 7

Pim

The heavy rains caused the roof to leak in the corner of their room, and a constant *drip, drip, drip* had kept Alesa awake for a large portion of the night. Gretchen provided a bucket to hold the water, which only amplified the annoying sound. It had stopped in the early morning hours, yet even then, Alesa had not managed a heavy slumber.

Her restlessness allowed ample time to think. Oddly, her thoughts had shifted from self-pity and frustration over her enchantment, to wonderment about Pim and why her heart seemed to be leading her to him.

She had numerous questions in his regard, but posing them would not be easy.

She pushed her covers back, went to the window, and peered out at the rising sun. The storms had completely ceased, making it the perfect day for their journey home.

Farrah and their mother still slept, so Alesa quietly dressed and crept from the room. She tiptoed down the stairs and into the tavern. No one was about.

So unlike last night…

The door opened and Gretchen entered, toting a basket of eggs. "I see you are an early riser. I have yet to start the morning meal."

Alesa had no choice but to sing. "*To eat is not my need right now, I have no appetite. I wish to walk and appreciate all the beauty in my sight. If my mother should wake, and my sister, too, please tell them I have gone. I will not linger, and I vow to them, my return will be anon.*"

Gretchen stared as she sang, and when she finished, the dear lady grunted. "You make conversing *interesting*. I will give your message to your family. Take care on your walk."

Alesa curtsied in response and hastened out the door.

A rooster crowed from somewhere nearby, reminding her of the early hour. It was probably foolish to set her feet on the path to the alchemist's cottage. Even so, an internal pull drew her in that direction.

She arrived at the curious green door and pressed her ear to it. The sound of shuffling feet within greeted her, and she smiled. Waldemar was awake.

Having no fear of rousing a possibly sleeping Pim, she thumped her fist against the door and waited patiently for Waldemar to open it.

"For the sake of heaven," he grumbled as he swung it wide. "Oh. It is *you*." He took her in from top to bottom. "You are no longer matted with rain, although your eyes are puffy." He wiggled his bony finger toward them. "Little sleep?"

She nodded. Extensive singing would come soon enough. She pointed into his cottage and questioned with her *puffy* eyes.

"It appears I have another Pim standing before me. Come in."

Alesa bravely crossed his threshold this time, knowing what oddities he kept inside. She no longer feared them. Being honest with herself, fear had almost left her, and she had become an emboldened woman.

Waldemar moved to his chair by the fire, slowly lowered into it, and lifted a steaming beverage from the table beside it. "My morning tea. Would you like some?"

She shook her head and put herself once again in front of his flickering fire.

He sipped his drink and peered up at her. "You seem quite at ease in my abode. When you came to me the first time, I sensed you did not want to be here at all. Why have you returned?"

Before answering, she paused a moment to look around the place, searching for signs of Pim. She noticed a shut door on the far side of the cottage. Perhaps he lay asleep in a bed behind it.

"*I came to ask you questions, about your servant, Pim. How came he to your service, and what will you share of him?*"

The old man chuckled. "I knew you were enthralled with him—and he with you." His eyes narrowed. "Do you intend to take him from my employ?"

"*I would not strip you of your loyal servant, dear old man. I only want to learn about his past and all I can.*"

"Because you care for him."

She twisted her fingers together and nodded. "*I do not understand it, I know him not at all. But something draws me to him, like a voice without a call.*"

"Oh, my. That is very profound—considering he is unable to call you to him." He set his cup aside, sat taller in his chair, and stroked his long beard. "I will tell you what you ask. Would you not be more comfortable sitting?" He gestured to a chair.

She smiled her appreciation, grabbed the chair, set it in front of him, and sat.

"As I told you yesterday, Pim came to me as a boy of seven. He was a pitiful lad, dirty and roaming the village, begging for food, as only he can. In silent earnestness. I inquired about him to those in the market, and I learned that his parents were travelers who abandoned him because of his impairments. Someone said his name was Pim, but I honestly believe they simply heard him referred to as *him* and misunderstood. Regardless, every child deserves a name, so I used it. Of course, he cannot hear it uttered and pays no mind to what I call him."

The man gazed at the fire and softly smiled. "I have grown fond of him, and I hope he sees me as a good father. But I am aging, and all of my attempts at finding the means to extend life have been to no avail. I tend to worry what will become of him when I pass." His attention returned to Alesa. "Now that you have come, perhaps I can stop worrying, hmm?"

A heated blush crept into her cheeks.

As before, Waldemar chuckled, then grew quite serious. "Pim is exceedingly intelligent—aside from his inability to read. That, however, is not uncommon. Only a handful of men in the realm have mastered the craft, but Pim has other fine attributes. He is an accomplished cook, gardener, and craftsman. He can wield a saw and hammer like no other." He leaned forward. "Pim would be a suitable husband to a woman with an enchanted voice. He would never grow weary of hearing you."

Husband? She widened her eyes and sat back in her chair.

Waldemar waved his hand. "Do not look so surprised, precious girl. You both are of that age. I see it as a proper fit and an answer to all of our troubles."

"So, you want me to take him from you? Is that the words I hear? I thought you feared of losing, the one you hold so dear?"

"I do not mean for you to whisk him off this day. Get to know the boy and make certain your heart has properly guided you. Comprehending mere gestures can be a challenge, and if your heart is not devoted and persistent, you will come to resent him."

He picked up his teacup and took another sip. "What happened to the young woman who was so mournfully determined to rid herself of her enchantment? You are not as hesitant to use your voice any longer. And what of your mother and sister? Where are they?"

"I cannot change my station, so accepting it is best. As for my loving family, in Gretchen's care, they remain at rest."

"Brilliant," Waldemar muttered. "I enjoy listening to your rhymes. Sadly, Pim will not benefit from them, but you have other qualities he will *relish*." The man said the word with a naughty smirk and jiggled his brows.

"Your thoughts do surely shame you, old man that you may be!" She leered and shook a finger. *"I may be young, but not naïve, your meaning I do see!"*

"Yes, I am old, but I am not dead. Can a man not appreciate the beauty of a lovely young woman? Besides, being Pim's father, I want him to happily embrace all the good life can bring—including the love of an exceptional woman. He was not afforded that in his youth."

She had been inclined to slap him for his crude remark and flirtatious gesture, yet his newest statement warmed her to the core. *"You are forgiven for the words you spoke so carelessly, but mind yourself from here on out, and a gentleman please be."*

"I will. I promise."

The door on the other side of the room opened, and her heart jumped when Pim walked in wearing a long nightshirt. His hair stuck out in disarray, and his eyelids were nearly shut. He yawned, stretched, and scratched his behind.

"Oh, dear," Waldemar mumbled.

Alesa snapped herself around and faced the fire. From the corner of her vision, she caught the alchemist digging into his pocket. He withdrew a bean and pelted it at Pim.

Alesa braved turning just enough to see Pim's reaction.

The instant he saw her, his eyes grew as large as a full moon. He whipped his body in a circle, went back into the bedroom, and slammed the door behind him.

Waldemar giggled like a little girl.

"*Embarrassment should not be a thing to humor you. Poor Pim will likely never come again into this room!*"

"You do not know him well." Waldemar's laughter subsided, and he thrummed his fingers on his lap.

Very few moments had passed when the bedroom door reopened and Pim reappeared, fully dressed. He had even combed his hair. With his head high, he strode across the floor and stood next to his master. Pim opened his arms wide and stared at the man in question.

Waldemar pushed up from his chair, motioned for Pim to sit, and made an extremely lude gesture. Alesa stared in shock, then calmed once she realized that his motions told Pim that he needed to use the privy.

With that, the old man shuffled off and went out the door, leaving her alone with Pim.

Purposefully?

Without a doubt.

Pim licked his lips, and his leg rapidly bounced. Nervous, to say the least. She, however, felt oddly comfortable with him.

Yet, how does one start a conversation with a man who cannot hear?

He looked right at her, awkwardly smiled, and turned his head. Abruptly, he stood and gazed down at her. He pointed at her face, gestured as if eating, then questioned with his eyes and rubbed his belly.

She understood. He wanted to know if she was hungry. She was, but even if she still had no appetite, she would encourage him to cook since Waldemar claimed him to be good at it. Doing something *normal* might take away his discomfort.

She smiled and nodded.

Pim lit up like a blazing beacon and scurried off. He disappeared into the same room he had gotten the tea from, and she assumed it to be a kitchen. Unlike her own home where everything but the bedrooms was in one room, Waldemar's cottage had several separate areas. Being that the main room had so many dead creatures lying about, she deemed it best he did not cook there.

She calmly sat and gathered her thoughts, and soon, the scent of frying bacon surrounded her. Her stomach growled.

Another more powerful noise drew her attention. A flurry of raised voices came from outside. Alesa went to open the door to discover the reason when Waldemar walked in. She peered beyond him to the street where a number of people had gathered, all loudly speaking.

Waldemar took hold of her hand. "It has finally happened. King Lorin has banished Zeborah."

Alesa's heart raced, and she begged with her eyes for him to say more.

"The town crier stated that Prince Chadwick insisted on the banishment. The prince came upon Zeborah, who was muttering strange words and was about to pour the contents of a vial into the maid, Jenessa's, mouth. Jenessa lay in a deep slumber and did not see the witch. Prince Chadwick smacked the vial from her hand, and it shattered on the floor. Had Zeborah administered the potion, I fear her enchantment would have been the evilest she had ever cast. She claims love for the prince, but Jenessa is *his* true love. His feelings for the low-statured maid drove Zeborah to cruelty in a fit of jealousy. Just as she did to you and the others she enchanted."

Alesa rubbed across her aching heart. She felt utterly horrible for even considering that the prince had been toying with Jenessa's emotions. He had saved her from Zeborah's wickedness, and more than likely, he had kept Jenessa in a lowly position to make Zeborah believe she mattered not to him. All along, he had been protecting the lowly maid.

The memory of the bitter taste that covered Alesa's tongue the night of *her* enchantment came to mind. *"Will Zeborah seek out vengeance to those who cast her out? Am I to fear her wrath will come and worsen my vocal bout?"*

"When one is banished, they cannot reenter Shanavar. I questioned the town crier in depth, and Zeborah was escorted by armed guards to the border. If she comes again into our lands, she will be killed." He tightened his hold on Alesa's hand and deeply peered into her eyes. "Never stray from Shanavar."

She clutched onto him, hugged him, and kissed his cheek. *"I must go and tell my mother and my sister what has come. Please tell dear Pim I will return, but for now I have to run. I care for him, indeed, I do. Pim rests within my heart. When I come back, we will find a way to never have to part."*

"Do you truly mean that, young one?"

She smiled and patted over her heart. Some things could not be fully explained, but the alchemist donned a tender expression, and she knew he understood.

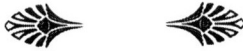

❦   ❦

"Alesa…" Her mother hastened to her side the instant she stepped into the tavern. "I have been so worried, yet I knew not where to look for you. Why did you leave? Was it to simply *walk*, as Gretchen told me?"

Alesa opened her mouth to sing her response when the door burst open behind her.

"The town crier decreed that Zeborah has been banished from Shanavar!" the man shouted to everyone within. "She tried to bewitch Jenessa, Prince Chadwick's love!" He raced out again, likely to spread the news further.

Farrah stood from where she was eating and joined Alesa and their mother. "Did you hear? At last, it has come to pass!"

Mumbled chatter arose from all the patrons in the establishment who had gathered to partake of the morning meal.

Alesa gestured for her family to go back to the long board for a more private conversation. They seated themselves, but before she could sing a note, Sir Jonas approached them.

"Such blessed news." His features almost glowed with joy. "I can return to King Lorin without fear. True, I may be reprimanded for my disloyalty, but my family will be safe. That is all that matters." He looked directly at Alesa. "I spoke with Ida about the possibility of employing you to help with our son. You see, my wife is with child again, and it will be difficult in the coming days for her to manage her own ailments *and* our fussy boy. Will you consider it? You have a gentleness about you that will benefit us all."

Alesa's mind spun. She had promised to be with Pim when needed. Could she fulfill that vow *and* tend a child? *"I am honored by your offer, and your kindness, loyal knight. But I ask you give me time for consideration, if you might?"*

"Of course. When you have decided, come to the castle. We reside there—unless the king chooses to dismiss me. If that happens…"

"You have no cause to worry. King Lorin is quite good. He shall cast fair judgment, as any ruler should."

Sir Jonas gave her a low, honorable bow. "As I said, your gentle manner would benefit us all. Good day to you." He nodded at her, then respectfully did the same to her mother and Farrah and walked off.

Alesa huffed.

Farrah grasped her arm. "Why did you not say yes? He would *pay* you. And you no longer have to fear seeing Zeborah in the castle. Aside from the troubles with your voice, your life could take a wonderful turn."

How could she answer simply, with such a complex situation?

Her mother stared at her with incredibly sad, confused eyes. The dear woman wanted only the best for her, and apparently, she believed Alesa planned to discard an opportunity that would provide that very thing.

"I am no longer troubled with the way I use my voice. Or even with the fact Zeborah took away my choice. As for the knight's fine offer, I am quite confused. My heart has led me elsewhere, to a man who was abused." She kept her volume low, so as not to draw attention. *"As a boy, he was abandoned and had no love and care. Until the alchemist saved him from a life of great despair. But Waldemar is aging and fears he soon will die. Pim needs someone to help him, and to love him by and by."*

Her mother clutched her bosom. "Oh, good heavens. You want us to take in that mute?"

Alesa laid her hand atop her mother's. "*He may not speak or hear at all, to me that matters not. Our hearts have somehow become joined, without it being sought.*"

"You *love* him?"

"*In time perhaps, a love will grow, but only if we see. We must spend time together to find out what will be.*"

Farrah twisted some hair around her finger. "He is handsome, although…" She blew out a breath. "Would you not prefer someone who can speak?"

Alesa softly smiled. "*To talk is not the only way we get our words across. Of anyone, I know it, from the way I suffered loss. I want my heart to show me why it leads me to Pim's care. And understand the meaning of the feelings that I bear.*"

"A tug of the heart…" her mother muttered. "I felt that with your father. You are indeed ripe for marriage. I simply do not feel that Pim is suitable. What can he provide you?"

Alesa appreciated her mother's concern. "*His master claims him gifted in many different arts. He gardens, cooks, and hammers, and he has a lot of smarts. I know not of his wealth, but assume it to be none, yet what we need will surely come from songs that I have sung.*"

"Or from tending Sir Jonas's babe," Farrah eagerly added. "But…is being with Pim what you truly want?"

Alesa shrugged. "*Time will reveal my surety and his as well, you see. For what I feel is only half of what I hope will be.*"

Her mother sighed, but immediately lifted her head high. "I presume you will want to make many a trek to the alchemist's cottage?"

Alesa's face warmed as she nodded to her mother, but the heat in her cheeks did not come from embarrassment. The thought of spending time with Pim warmed her. It would be an adventure she relished, and one she intended to begin as soon as possible.

Jeanne Hardt

Epilogue

Blissful Acceptance

Alesa swayed with baby Jace, who slept soundly in her arms. Bo stretched out beside her on the grassy bank of the creek. He lay contentedly, likely because she had not attempted to bathe him.

On her other side, Pim sat, staring at the water.

Fortunately, Farrah had grown used to the idea of giving her and Pim the opportunity to spend time alone. She had stayed behind with their mother at the cottage. Alesa had been gone extensively, spending her days at the castle, and their mother needed more help in their gardens, as well as with the few mending jobs that came their way.

Alesa glanced over at Pim, wishing she could read his thoughts. It had been two months since Waldemar had taken ill and passed away. He had left his cottage and belongings to Pim— along with a scant amount of money. Surely, Pim missed the dear old man.

She was glad Pim felt comfortable on the occasions that he stayed with her and her family and slept on a pallet on the floor, but most often, he remained at the alchemist's cottage. Either being near to the memories of Waldemar helped him, or the deep emptiness his death had left behind continued to hurt. She had witnessed many different emotions from Pim since the alchemist's death, and conveying *precise* feelings seemed difficult for him to convey. Still, they had a lifetime to learn each other's frame of mind.

In two weeks, they would be married, and she hoped to ease all of Pim's suffering. Much would change for both of them. Thankfully, he had agreed to sell Waldemar's cottage and build their own closer to the castle. All of the new mothers there had been made aware of Alesa's soothing voice, and they kept her well employed. Her own mother certainly appreciated the money it brought in, keeping food on the family table. No longer did she express any sort of annoyance at Alesa's never-ending vocalizing, or the gestures that accompanied it.

No rumors had arisen of Zeborah attempting to regain entry into the realm, and now that Alesa had Pim in her life, she contentedly remained in Shanavar—even though Mount Ashalon often beckoned her. Journeying there was not to be, but certainly, she and Pim would create their own adventures right at home.

She tapped Pim's leg to draw his attention. Waldemar had left behind sacks full of dried beans, but Alesa hoped to never have to use them. She wanted every touch between her and Pim to be gentle.

He looked at her with the love she had become used to seeing, and he questioned with his kind eyes. Her heart pattered harder. Every day she gave thanks that she had listened to it and followed it to Pim.

She pointed at him, then at herself, and finally at her own smiling mouth, asking if he was happy being with her.

His loving gaze deepened. He tenderly threaded his fingers into her hair, leaned forward, and placed a soft kiss on her lips. She blissfully sighed.

Enough said.

Having her speaking voice stripped away was not the curse she had initially believed it to be. Pim had no voice at all, but she could share hers, allowing them both to benefit from it. Zeborah had told her to wear it well and may have meant for the enchantment to be a cruel, ill-intended gesture. Instead, the sorceress had indeed given her a blessed gift.

Like the beautiful birds Alesa so often admired, she would live out her days expressing herself with an endless song...

About the author

Jeanne Hardt has always been involved in the arts in one form or fashion. In 1993, she moved to Tennessee from North Idaho to pursue a career in music and acting, but she soon found her true passion…writing.

She writes historical, contemporary, and young adult fiction as well as fantasy.

Jeanne still lives in Tennessee with her husband and her writing buddy, Jax, a spunky Chihuahua mix.

www.jeannehardt.net